# A Pirate's Mother Goose

## (And Other Rhymes)

Nancy I. Sanders

pictures by Colin Jack

Albert Whitman & Company
Chicago, Illinois

To Captain Adorable, our grandson Ryan,
the cutest pirate to ever sail the seven seas.
With love from Grandma Nancy
*For this child we prayed. 1 Samuel 1:27*

To Gabriel Cutlas Jack and Mad Eli Jack
Love, Dad

Library of Congress Cataloging-in-Publication
data is on file with the publisher.


Pictures by Colin Jack
Published in 2015 by Albert Whitman & Company
ISBN 978-0-8075-6559-9


Printed in China
10 9 8 7 6 5 4 3 2 1 HH 20 19 18 17 16 15

Design by Ellen Kokontis

For more information about Albert Whitman & Company,
visit our web site at www.albertwhitman.com.

N
W
E
S
Bay of
Bo Peep
King
Cole
Cavern
Mother
Hubbard
Mountain
Humpty
Dumpty
Isle

# Rub-a-dub-dub

Rub-a-dub-dub,
three swabs in a tub,
and who do ye think they be?
The ship's cook, the first mate,
and Blackbeard the pirate
sailing the salty sea.

# Sing a Song of Hardtack

(Sing a Song of Sixpence)

Sing a song of hardtack,
a pirate's daily grub.
Eat it in your hammocks.
Munch it in the tub.
If ye don't love hardtack
for morning, noon, and night,
better not be sailin' off
in pirate ships tonight!

# One Misty, Moisty Morning

One misty, moisty morning,
when cloudy was the weather,
I chanced to meet a pirate
with a peacock feather.
He began to compliment,
and I began to grin.
Ahoy there, mate! And ahoy there, mate!
And ahoy there, mate, again!

# Pretty Polly Parrot

(Wee Willy Winkie)

Pretty Polly Parrot
flies through the town
in all the houses
upstairs and down,
peeping through the windows,
squawking through the locks,
"Be the children safe in bed?
There be pirates at the docks!"

# Diddle Diddle Dumpling, Buccaneer John

(Diddle Diddle Dumpling, My Son John)

Diddle diddle dumpling, Buccaneer John
went to bed with his britches on.
One boot off and one boot on.
Diddle diddle dumpling, Buccaneer John.

# Peg-Leg Jack Horner

(Little Jack Horner)

Peg-Leg Jack Horner
sat in a corner,
giving his treasure some thought.
He pulled out his map,
then tugged on his cap,
and said, "Blimey! *X* marks the spot!"

# Rock-a-by, Pirate

(Rock-a-by, Baby)

Rock-a-by, pirate, anchored at dock,
when the wind blows, the crow's nest will rock;
when the mast breaks, the crow's nest will fall,
down will come pirate, crow's nest and all.

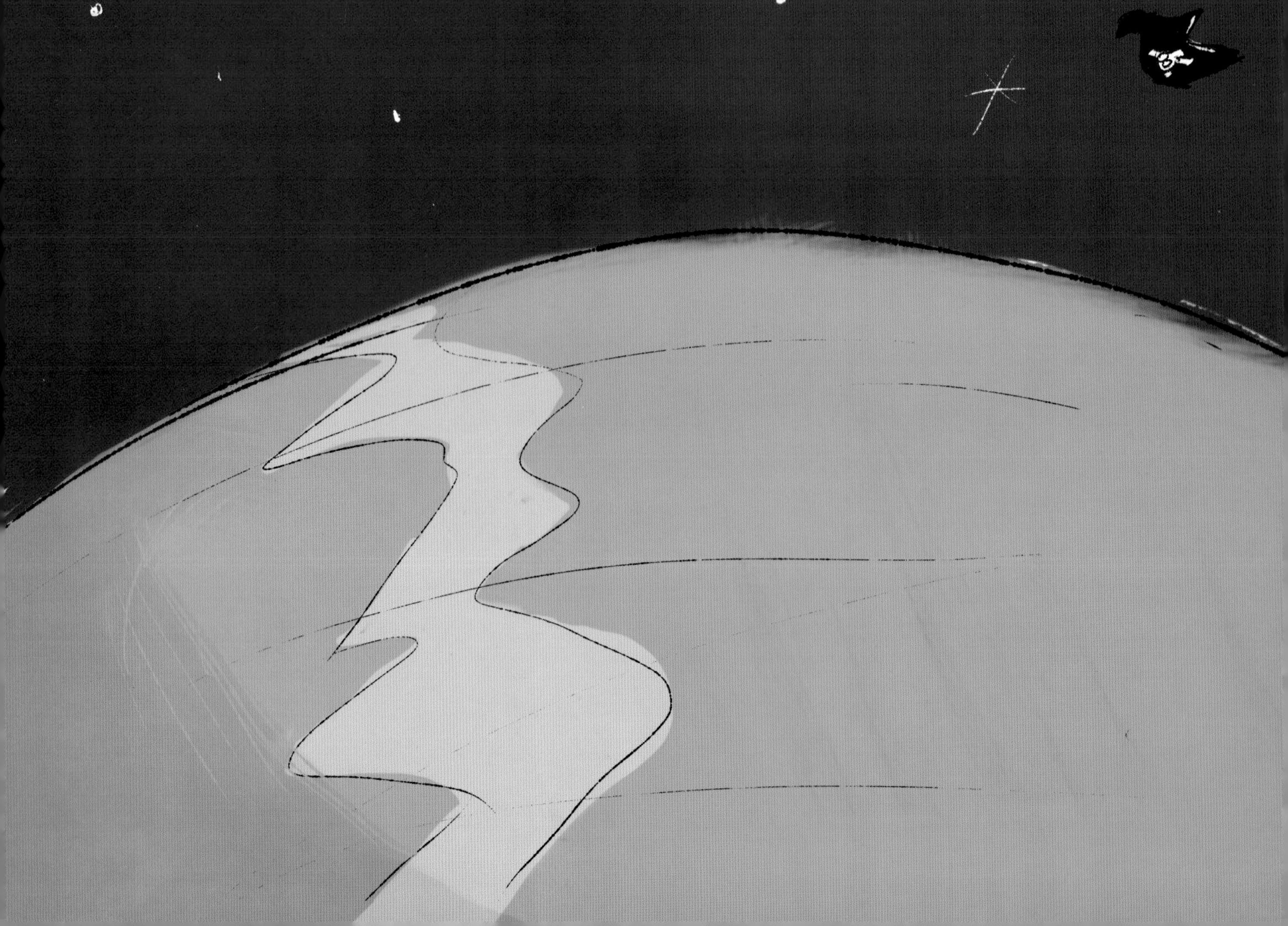

# The Pirate Queen

(The Queen of Hearts)

The pirate queen,
she wore a ring,
all on a summer's day;
Scurvy Dog Dean,
he stole that ring,
and took it clean away.

The pirate king
called for the ring.
"Or walk the plank!" he roared.
Scurvy Dog Dean
brought back the ring
and vowed he'd steal no more.

# One, Two, Sail into the Blue

(One, Two, Buckle My Shoe)

One, two,
sail into the blue.
Three, four,
drop anchor off shore.
Five, six,
grab shovels and picks.
Seven, eight,
bury the crate.
Nine, ten,
search for treasure again!

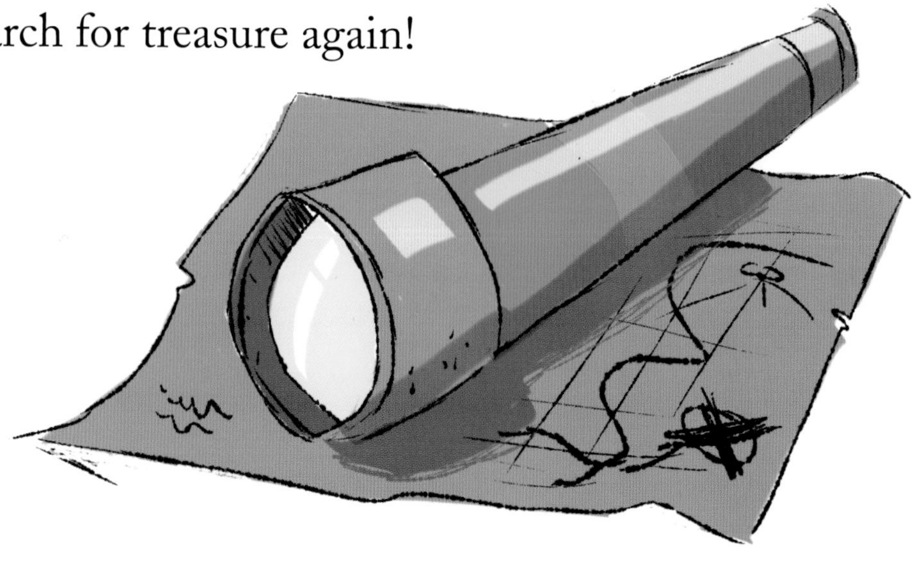

# Captain Jack

(Jack Sprat)

Captain Jack could read a map.
His mate knew how to measure.
And so between the two of them,
they found the buried treasure.

# Hey, Diddle Diddle

Hey, diddle diddle,
the mate played his fiddle.
The cabin boy danced a jig.
The pirate king laughed
to see such sport,
while the scalawags waltzed in the brig.

# Hardtack

(Pease Porridge Hot)

Hardtack when it's hot.
Hardtack when it's cold.
Hardtack when it's in the pot,
nine days old.

Ye won't like it hot.
Ye won't like it cold.
Ye won't like it in the pot,
nine days old.

# Little Miss Pirate

(Little Miss Muffet)

Little Miss Pirate
sat very quiet,
ladylike all the day.
But when the captain would shout,
“Hoist the main sails!”
Miss Pirate yelled,

# There Was an Old Sea Dog

## (There Was an Old Woman Who Lived in a Shoe)

There was an old sea dog who sailed the briny blue.
He had so many riches he didn't know what to do.
He bought an old sea chest with a golden doubloon,
then buried his treasure in a secret lagoon.

# Ye Can Talk Like Pirates Talk

(London Bridge Is Falling Down)

Ye can talk like pirates talk,
pirates talk, pirates talk.
Ye can talk like pirates talk.
Aye, aye, matey!

When yer happy say, "Yo-ho!"
Say, "Yo-ho!" Say, "Yo-ho!"
When yer happy say, "Yo-ho!"
Aye, aye, matey!

When yer mad say, "Walk the plank!
Walk the plank! Walk the plank!"
When yer mad say, "Walk the plank!"
Aye, aye, matey!

When yer working say, "Heave ho!"
Say, "Heave ho!" Say, "Heave ho!"
When yer working say, "Heave ho!"
Aye, aye, matey!

When yer finished say, "Shipshape!"
Say, "Shipshape!" Say, "Shipshape!"
When yer finished say, "Shipshape!"
Aye, aye, matey!

When yer shocked say, "Blow me down!
Blow me down! Blow me down!"
When yer shocked say, "Blow me down!"
Aye, aye, matey!

When ye get there say, "Ahoy!"
Say, "Ahoy!" Say, "Ahoy!"
When ye get there say, "Ahoy!"
Aye, aye, matey!

When ye leave say, "Anchors aweigh!
Anchors away! Anchors aweigh!"
When ye leave say, "Anchors aweigh!"
Aye, aye, matey!

# Yo-Ho, Pirate!

(Baa, Baa, Black Sheep)

Yo-ho, pirate!
Have ye any gold?
Yes, sir! Yes, sir!
Three bags told.

One for the captain,
one for the cook,
one for the buccaneer
with peg leg and hook.

Yo-ho, pirate!
Have ye any gold?
Yes, sir! Yes, sir!
Three bags told.

# One Eye Patch

(Three Blind Mice)

One eye patch.
One eye patch.
Spyglass and sword.
Spyglass and sword.
If ye want to dress up like a buccaneer,
ye wear a scarf and a ring in yer ear.
Ye swagger around in yer pirate's gear,
and one eye patch.

# There Was a Crooked Crew

(There Was a Crooked Man)

There was a crooked crew, who sailed a crooked mile.
They found a crooked gold piece upon a crooked isle.
They bought a crooked cat, and got a crooked goat,
and they all lived together in a leaky, crooked boat.

# Raise the Jolly Roger High

(Twinkle, Twinkle Little Star)

Raise the Jolly Roger high
up the mast and watch it fly.
Black flag waving in the breeze
shows we're masters of the seas.
Raise the Jolly Roger high.
Hoist our colors to the sky.

# Pat-a-Cake

Pat-a-cake, pat-a-cake,
pirate king!
Bake me a cake
with a golden ring.
Roll it, and pat it,
and mark it with a P.
Put it in the oven
for the pirates and me.

# Cabin Boy Blue

## (Little Boy Blue)

Cabin boy blue,
come swab the deck.
The tar is all sticky.
The poop deck's a wreck.
Where is the boy
who must work for his keep?
He's inside a barrel,
fast asleep.

The Little Old
Woman's Shoe
Peter
Piper's
Peak
Strait of
Simple Simon

# Cabin Boy Blue

(Little Boy Blue)

Cabin boy blue,
come swab the deck.
The tar is all sticky.
The poop deck's a wreck.
Where is the boy
who must work for his keep?
He's inside a barrel,
fast asleep.

# This Little Pirate

(This Little Piggy)

This little pirate sailed to China.
This little pirate stayed home.
This little pirate found treasure.
This little pirate found none.
And this little pirate cried, “Shiver me timbers!”
all the way home.

The Little Old Woman's Shoe
Peter Piper's Peak
Strait of Simple Simon